HAUNTED

A STARLITE MYSTERY

THE STARLITE SUPERNATURAL MYSTERY SERIES

RAY & MICHELE FRASER

Hidden Door Press
Los Angeles, CA

Edited by Kristie Wagner
thebookwyrmsshelf@gmail.com

Cover design by Michele Fraser

❦ Created with Vellum

CHAPTER I
IT'S IN THE CARDS

My name is Brett. I'm a salesman for a major office equipment manufacturer. As such, I naturally have the gift of gab and love to talk. I had just closed a nice order for a variety of equipment. That meant a good commission would be coming my way. If there is anything that loosens my lips and encourages conversation, it's knowing that I made some money. So, it's not unusual for me to have a cordial conversation with purchasing agents after closing an order.

During one particular discussion with a buyer, the clerk, who was sitting nearby, interrupted. "Do you mind if I tell you about my house?" Judy inquired looking at me.

"No. Not at all." I replied glancing at the buyer with a shrug.

"It's haunted." Judy blurted out.

The other woman gasped.

I wasn't ready for that! "Haunted? Really? That's interesting, but why would you tell me?"

She shrugged, "I don't know. I just felt like I should."

Judy had been sitting within earshot of our chat. Of course, once it got started, anyone was welcome to join in, but a haunted house? And why me? My interest in the paranormal was seriously limited. In fact, when you work for one of the most conservative and professional corporations in the world, personal interests and hobbies, particularly those that hovered just outside the realm of normalcy, were not topics open for discussion with clients. Still, I was intrigued. To fully explain my position, I'll need to start this story a couple of months earlier.

As I mentioned, I work for a major office supplier. I live in Ann Arbor, Michigan, and work in Jackson County, some 40 miles to the west of Ann Arbor. My employer is a wonderful but tough company to work for. Unless you have a doctor's note, they want you at work. Weather conditions were not considered a dire emergency. Unfortunately, the Washtenaw and Jackson County Road commissions were not as concerned about my attendance as my boss. Often in the winter, the freeway between Ann Arbor and Jackson was neglected, becoming a serious threat.

On this particular day, it was the dead of winter and approximately a month prior to my sale date. The roads were treacherous and covered with black ice. Fortunately, one of our company's best service technicians also lived near me in Ann Arbor, and it was her turn to drive. On those winter days when the roads were bad and neither Barb nor I figured we would spend a great deal of time out of the office on sales or service calls, we would carpool and spend the day in the local office doing paperwork. This minimized our risks of being involved in an accident on unsafe roads. It also prevented the need to hire a helicopter to ensure we fulfilled our company's attendance requirements.

Barb owned a large home from which she rented rooms to the University of Michigan students. That day, it was also her turn to cook dinner for the house. The return ride was slow and arduous. The thought of going home and cooking a meal was not a happy thought, so I was glad when she invited me to stay for dinner. Her house was home to several 70s-era students. Most were too inexperienced to have refined their goals into what someone would call a successful life plan. Life was about school, catching a buzz, and attending the Ark, an upscale music house near campus where many soon-to-be famous musicians had performed on their route to stardom. With the car safely parked in front of the house, I followed Barb in and sat in anticipation of a home-cooked meal that I didn't have to prepare.

"It'll be about an hour," Barb announced to the group.

That seemed like a long time, but the television was broadcasting reruns of Star Trek, and in those days, it was still a novelty. We sat watching as Captain Kirk and Spock tried to thwart the latest alien invasion. As the show went to a commercial break, I noticed a deck of cards sitting on a small table. My first thought was perhaps a game of cards would help pass the time, yet when I picked them up, they had the most unusual pictures on them. There wasn't a heart, diamond, spade, or club among them. I incorrectly assumed that someone from the house would know how to play, so I picked them up, shuffled them slightly, and began dealing them out. After everyone had a few, I saw and heard Barb rushing to where we sat.

"Hey, those aren't playing cards; they're fortune-telling cards."

"Fortune telling?" I asked, "How do they work?"

"Let's set these aside and I'll tell you later," she offered, taking the cards quickly from our hands and then carefully restacking them into the deck.

Dinner was wonderful, but a blur. I wanted to know about the cards. Finally, with all the dishes cleared, Barb got the cards and brought them to the table, spreading them out before us.

"These are Tarot cards. Sorry I was so abrupt earlier. I'm a little protective of them because I'm still learning. They're used to forecast a person's future." She pulled out a small book that came with the deck. On the pages were the meanings of the cards and several different placement spreads.

"Can I try it?" I requested eagerly.

Barb was a bit hesitant but finally agreed. "But no joking around. You've got to be serious."

I thought. *How can I be serious about something I don't even understand?*

My first reading was for a young man who went by the nickname, Cas. To my astonishment, he acknowledged many of the things I foresaw coming into his future.

"That's like far out, man. How did you know that shit?"

I didn't know and said as much. "It's all in the cards," I answered. With a small measure of success under my belt, being serious was becoming easier.

The little book that came with the deck had multiple meanings for each card. I simply related the meaning that I felt applied to the person I was reading. Before long, I'd read for most of the people in the house and it was time to call it a night.

"Thanks for dinner. By the way, where did you buy those cards?"

"Borders," she revealed. "In the Occult section."

The rest of the evening was a time of confusion and scrambled thoughts. Was it really possible that I could see into the future for people? It had been as though someone was guiding my impressions as I paged through the book.

After a virtually sleepless night, I arose early, dressed, and drove to work. However, on my way, I took a slight detour and headed for Borders Bookstore in downtown Ann Arbor. After a quick search, I found my only option, a deck of Rider Waite Tarot cards, complete with an instruction book.

At a rest area just before Jackson, I parked and cracked the deck of cards open. One by one, I took the cards out and looked up their meaning, trying to place each one into my memory banks for future reference. This was going to be a major undertaking. There were seventy-eight cards, four different suits, and multiple meanings for each card. *How would anyone be able to remember all that information?*

When I arrived at work, Barb was already there.

"Finally," she announced. "I've been waiting to talk to you."

"Really? Why?"

"You caused quite a stir. No one could stop talking about the readings. You flipped people out."

"That's cool," I replied. "In a good way, I hope."

"Yes, in fact, it looks like you may have uncovered a gift," she smiled. "If you're interested, I think you should keep working at it."

CHAPTER 2
THE SEMINAR

B arb's encouragement was just what I needed. For the next couple of weeks, I practiced with the cards, doing readings for family and friends, and gaining confidence with each successful interpretation.

On the day of my sales call, I was surprised and intrigued to hear about the haunted house. I just didn't know how to react, since I'd never encountered one before.

I decided to call Barb and ask her to dinner to discuss the new situation. Fortunately, she agreed and suggested we meet at Pizza Bob's.

Barb shared my curious enthusiasm and inquired right after we ordered, "Now, what about this lady with the haunted house?"

"That's a good question. I'm not sure what she's looking for, but I told her I was interested in helping if I could. She was gonna check with her husband and see if there was a time when I could come over. Wanna go?"

"I'm not sure." Barb took a deep breath and probed, "What did she say was happening?"

"She has an 8-year-old son and a 14-year-old daughter. They

have both seen the face of a man in their second-floor bedroom windows and a full apparition. Also, they have a large ceramic owl that sits on a stereo. Every morning it's moved off the top and placed in the middle of the living room floor. Plus, they're hearing strange sounds, mostly from the basement."

"Do you think it's a joke?"

"No, she was definitely serious. She said her husband's terrified and they don't have any idea what to do, other than move. They had apparently thought about, but decided it wasn't an option."

"Well, I don't know anything about ghosts."

"Me neither," I answered, "But it would be cool to check out, and I thought maybe the Tarot cards could give us some guidance."

She quickly responded, "I guess I'll go and see this for myself."

Her reply didn't surprise me. She was intelligent, adventurous, and resourceful. We would make a good team. Now all I had to do was wait to hear from the homeowner.

The next day was Friday, and I received a call from Judy. The following weekend, her children would stay overnight at a friend's house, and Saturday would be the perfect time for me to come. I asked if a friend would be welcome to join and she assured me that would be fine.

I called Barb. "Let's do Pizza Bob's. The lady got in touch with me."

I agreed to go to Barb's house after work since she lived close to the restaurant. After a short walk, we placed our order and sat waiting for our pie to be ready. During these quiet moments, I restated my conversation with Judy and attempted to formulate a plan for our visit. I had no clue what to expect and even less of an idea of what to do. I didn't think that we would run into Casper, the friendly ghost, but if we did, I couldn't possibly be prepared for the meeting. My plan was to cram in as much knowledge about the Tarot as I could between now and then. Once in the house, I'd do a card spread and see what they told us.

Barb got up and walked to the bulletin board near the door where university activities were posted for students to see. "Look at this," she urged, pointing to a flier.

I joined her as she read aloud. "ESP Seminar. Kresge Hall. 8:00 PM Friday. Admission is free." She looked my way. "Do you wanna go?"

"Sure."

Extra Sensory Perception sounded intriguing, and I had no plans for Friday night. Hopefully the roads would stay clear and we could drive home from Jackson to Ann Arbor in time to make the seminar.

Friday dawned clear and cold. The forecast was calling for no snow that day or evening. I breathed a sigh of relief. What the heck was an ESP seminar? Was it some form of mind control? Communicating without words? I didn't know, but I was certain I was going to find out.

My answering machine indicated Barb had called. I ditched my business suit and opted for a pair of jeans and a red polo shirt. I planned to arrive at her house at 7:00 for the brief walk to the seminar. Barb was never one to be late, and this day was no exception. We arrived at approximately 7:15. Though this was a large hall, it was mostly filled by the time we arrived. We took seats near the back and waited for the lecture to begin.

Promptly at 8:00, two gentlemen walked on stage and introduced themselves as professors from Duke University in North Carolina. They began giving us the itinerary for the evening, plus information about studies they had conducted involving ESP. The first half of the seminar would be spent explaining what they knew about it, plus their personal experiences researching ESP and the paranormal. The second half would involve an audience participation demonstration. I found the information and descriptions fascinating but couldn't see a correlation between me and Extra Sensory Perception.

At approximately 9:00, the gentleman who had been offstage during the first portion returned. "We are now going to select eleven people from the audience for an actual ESP presentation."

He described what they were going to do as "sending and receiving." One person would be asked to think in great detail about someone they knew. This person would be the sender. The remaining ten people would voice feelings and thoughts they believed were received from the sender about that individual. All responses would be tape-recorded by the organizers for verification by the sender at the end of the demonstration.

The man began picking people around the auditorium. I sat in anticipation of what was to transpire until I heard him say, "You in the red shirt."

As people began making their way to the stage, Barb proclaimed, "He's pointing at you."

"Me?"

I didn't know anything about this stuff. Still, I'd been called, so I slowly made my way to the aisle and down the stairs to the stage. We all sat around a large conference table. They selected one lady as the sender. She sat at the head of the table to my left. A conference microphone was placed in the center so they didn't miss a word. They gave the sender a few moments to think of someone and, upon her hand signal, people began giving out their impressions of the person she held in her thoughts.

For several moments, my mind was a blank page, and I received nothing. Then, quickly, images started appearing in my mind. She was thinking of a woman who wore a uniform and who was a long way from home. It seemed that she had just arrived where she was and wouldn't be going home for quite some time. The last impression I had was of a large gray eagle statue. Shortly after, I would find out how important that was when the demonstration concluded.

I sat in anticipation to see if anything I had perceived had been accurate. What followed completely blew my mind. The lady had been thinking of her sister, who was in the Air Force. She had recently been assigned to Ramstein Air Base in Germany and wouldn't be returning home for two years. I was flabbergasted! How was it possible to sense all of that? However, the best was yet to come.

When I was in the Army, I was stationed in Baumholder, Germany, only forty miles from Ramstein. Approximately every two months, I would drive my tracked vehicle to the base for training maneuvers with the Air Force. The pilots used us as targets to practice their bombing runs. We would drive into the designated area and the pilots would attempt to drop fifty-pound bags of flour on us to improve their accuracy. We had taken part in this drill many times.

Ramstein Air Base has two-way traffic at its entrance, with a grass median separating the lanes. Sitting just outside the guard gate, in the center of the median, was a large gray eagle monument I looked at every time I entered or exited the base. How was it possible I had been shown this image? Where did the information come from? The guys running the seminar were also astonished, questioning if the sender and I knew each other, or had spoken before.

My fear was that I had stepped into some uncharted zone. I was a devout Christian, taught Sunday school, and sang in the choir. I hoped I hadn't crossed some dangerous line. Yet there was nothing negative about the information I received. I simply described the pictures I was seeing in my mind. Fortunately, or unfortunately, I didn't have a great deal of time to think about it. Our visit to Judy's house was only a week away. This experience would seem like mere child's play compared to what we would find in the haunted house.

CHAPTER 3
THE HOUSE

February is a cold and brutal month in Michigan. This year was no exception. As the days of the week passed, the temperature dropped lower and lower. Saturday, the temperature took a turn and warmed to an unexpected thirty degrees. The result was an ice storm with freezing rain, like none we had seen in recent years. The trip to Jackson that evening was perilous, with thick ice coating the road and windshield.

"If this wasn't so important, I'd turn around," I muttered under my breath.

Barb was a trooper and rode silently as I did my very best to keep the car on the road. Finally, our exit came up, and with a deep sigh and white knuckles, I edged off the freeway and turned in the direction of the haunted house. As imagined, the side streets weren't much better than the freeway, so we carefully crept down the path which led to the lakeside home of Dylan and Judy.

The house looked completely normal. What the heck did I know? I'd never seen a haunted house before. We were a few minutes late because of the weather. Judy and her husband Dylan were waiting at the door when we approached.

"Welcome," Dylan offered, extending his hand.

I shook it and smiled. "Thanks for having us. This is my friend, Barb."

"We sure hope you can help us." He remarked nervously.

"We hope so, too," I replied.

Dylan did not look like a guy who would be afraid of ghosts. He was broad-shouldered and rugged looking. We spent the next half hour talking about their experiences, which included loud banging from the basement, their children seeing images of a man in the second-story bedroom windows, and a large ceramic owl that mysteriously moved during the night and was found in the center of the living room floor every morning. I decided to be honest and relate my lack of experience with these types of situations, acknowledging my recent Tarot introduction and ESP exposure, but I included a firm promise that I would do everything I could to help solve their situation.

"We have no one else to call," Judy revealed. "You seem to be our only hope."

I started with a Tarot reading for the house to see what the cards would show. We took our seats around the dining-room table and I took my cards from their protective box. At the very moment they touched the table, a low moan was heard coming from the basement door, which was to my right and behind me. I looked at Barb as she took a deep breath and shook her head in disbelief.

Generally, I'm a hearty soul, but I was in uncharted waters. I had no clue what to expect nor any idea if the Tarot was related to spirit entities in any way, but I was sure we'd find out.

I shuffled the Tarot deck to prepare for a spread, then sat them down to cut into three stacks. When the cards touched the table, we again heard the low moan. Everyone turned to look at the basement door. It was not audibly human, but rather like the sound a large tree or wooden beam would make if put under extreme stress.

I cut the deck in three and restacked the cards. I picked up the top *representation card*, which was the Page of Swords. To me, it was symbolic of a younger male facing adversity.

"Who are you, and why are you in this house?" I demanded.

I placed the card face up on the table.

Boom! There was an unmistakable noise of something heavy striking one of the furnace pipes.

"That's the sound we hear," Dylan confirmed. "Only louder."

I turned the next card over. It was the Three of Swords. The position of this one reflected what energy was influencing the situation. *Not a good card,* I thought since it has a picture of a heart with three swords piercing it, usually indicating emotional distress. I placed it face-up on the first card and there was another rap from the basement, this time much louder. We all shared a glance. It was obvious tensions were rising.

"That's it. Just like that. Sometimes it goes on for hours." Judy added.

The noises were disturbing, but at least there were no ghosts flying around.

I decided to get organized and spoke to the spirit. "If the answer to my question is yes, give us a sound. If the answer is no, remain silent. Can you do that?"

We immediately heard a pinging noise from the basement.

I pushed for more information. "Does this have to do with matters of the heart?"

A cabinet door in the kitchen opened and slammed shut.

"Do you want us to help you?" I asked.

Three raps on the table gave us a jolt.

"It looks like we have a mystery to solve," I concluded.

It seemed like we were making progress. I was emboldened by our success and wanted to press on.

"Why don't we go into the basement?" I suggested with a hint of trepidation.

"If you think it will help," Dylan responded as stood to lead the way.

I followed, leaving the cards on the table.

The house had what is referred to as a Michigan basement. It was only tall enough to put in the necessary appliances, such as a furnace, hot water heater, sump pump, etc. A slab of concrete was poured in the center of the room where the furnace and water heater were mounted. Builders covered the remaining area of the basement floor in a large-stone gravel mix. The ceiling height was approximately five feet, so we wouldn't be able to stand.

"We can sit on the stairs," Judy offered.

Sounded like a great idea to me. Barb and I took seats directly behind her and Dylan.

It was then that I noticed their furnace was originally coal, now converted to an oil burner with large heat ducts. We used to call these octopus furnaces because of their appearance. A single heat source with arms branching out in several directions. *This is probably where the noises are coming from,* I thought.

Without the cards, how would I make contact with the spirit if indeed that was happening? My mind flashed to the ESP demonstration. There had been no cards there or any other props, yet the pictures came clearly and were recognizable. I searched my mind and to my surprise, images appeared.

"Are you male?" I began.

Several taps came from the door behind us.

"Were you killed in this house?" I continued with anticipation.

Three loud booms echoed off the walls.

I was beginning to feel confident.

"Were you buried in this basement?"

The sound of a bell rang out in thin air.

I felt a chill run through my body as the hair on the back of my neck stood up.

My mind went blank and I couldn't think of anything else to ask, but I believed we had established a means of communication with the spirit. One thing concerned me, during the entire questioning process, the furnace had been turning on and off about every two minutes.

"Does your furnace always do that?" I inquired.

They didn't answer. Judy had been noticeably silent since we sat down.

"Is everything alright?" I asked.

"Just fine," she whispered.

The furnace had calmed down some, but without warning or notice, the sump pump turned on.

Dylan began reciting the Lord's Prayer. Judy began weeping softly. Barb trembled nervously. Everyone was letting the events of the moment get to them. I tried to bring some reason back into our meeting.

"Dylan, it's only the sump pump!" I exclaimed.

"I know, but that pump hasn't worked in two years."

His response sent goosebumps through my body and told me it was time for Plan B.

The images I was seeing in my mind were very clear. We were not alone in the basement, and I sensed water.

"Was there ever a source of water in the basement?" I asked.

"Only the Cistern," Dylan replied.

Since we all were feeling a little disturbed. I suggested, "Let's go back upstairs and see if the cards will give us more information."

There was a moment's hesitation as we started to rise and leave. I heard a sound, like something heavy was being dragged across the basement gravel.

"Does anyone else hear the scraping sound?"

"It's like something is being moved." Judy voiced.

"Yeah, something large," Barb added.

That got us all moving up the stairs and we returned to the table, assuming our original seating positions. It felt good to be in a more comfortable environment.

"Do you think the spirit was causing all of that?"

Judy's question was a valid one, and I didn't know the answer. This was my first rodeo.

"Maybe we can figure something out. If nothing else, I'll do some research. Somebody has to know what is happening here and how to deal with it." I chuckled to myself. *Who the heck was I gonna call?*

"The priest said it might be an evil spirit. He wanted nothing to do with it." Dylan professed.

"I'm sure no ghost hunter, but I didn't feel anything negative. It seemed like we made contact with an intelligent entity who had lost their way and needed help. I have no doubt this is going to get a lot more complicated before we're through. So, right now, we can stop or go forward, your choice. I'm in till the end if you want."

"Do you think it will stop if we quit now?" Judy asked hopefully.

"I doubt it very much," I responded.

"Then I say we continue," she declared.

Dylan nodded in agreement. "If you're willing to stick it out, then I am, too."

"Good. Let's see what the Tarot has to say."

I picked up the deck and turned over the top card. The Star. A card from the Major Arcana section of the deck. It features a maiden pouring water on land and into a pond. The water was confirmed.

"Does everyone know what a cistern was used for?" They didn't reply.

So I explained, "Prior to running water, they were used to store rainwater for cleaning, washing, and irrigation. Most homes had them."

I asked the spirit, "Does the cistern have anything to do with you being here?"

A picture sitting nearby on the credenza fell forward, making us all gasp a breath and exchange glances. It seemed to be in direct response to my question.

The next card turned was The Lovers. A pattern was forming in my mind.

"Were you killed because of a woman?"

We heard three quick raps on the window.

"Did they put you in the cistern?"

There was a loud clap from the adjacent room and we all turned our heads but saw nothing.

"Was the woman involved with another man?"

A circling breeze seemed to fill the room as an unmistakable rat-a-tat-tat reverberated in our ears.

"Was she married?"

Another positive response.

"So, you were having an affair with another man's wife and he found out and killed you?"

Silence.

"Are you saying that you weren't having an affair?"

We heard a shrill whistle that made us all jump.

"Did her husband think you were having an affair with his wife?"

No answer.

"Correct me if I'm wrong. The lady's husband thought you were having an affair with his wife, so he killed you and placed you in the cistern?"

Again, silence.

When we were in the basement, I noticed someone had bricked up the cistern. Were you moved?"

The answer came in three distinctive strikes.

"Is the person who killed you still alive?"

Absolute quiet.

"Is the person who killed you dead?"

The reply was affirmative.

"Was he ever punished?"

Nothing.

"Will we be able to find out who did it?"

There was one soft tap, which I took as a maybe.

I turned over another card, representing the energy of the past. It was the King of Pentacles.

Everyone was looking at me. "Was the killer a rich and powerful man?"

The racket became loud and consistent. It sounded like I had touched a nerve.

"Last time it started like this, it didn't stop for two whole days." Judy insisted.

I looked at Barb. She shrugged her shoulders. What had I done? Did I piss off some wrongly murdered angry spirit and now these people were going to have to live with it? My thoughts went back to an old saying: *never send a boy to do a man's job.* I had no idea what to do next. I had hoped to help these folks, but it appeared to backfire.

"Judy. Can you find out who owned the house and possibly get a picture of it when it was first built? I feel like it has been significantly remodeled."

"I can try." She assured me.

"Perhaps if we can identify who did this, it will bring the spirit comfort and then you guys will get some peace, too."

The pounding on the pipes had become so unbearable that normal conversation could not be heard.

I looked at Dylan and spoke slowly so he could read my lips, "Is there someplace where we can talk?"

"Maybe on the deck," He motioned outside.

Their house was right on the water, and the deck hung over the lake. In Michigan, there are very few places that are colder than water's edge, at midnight. I was freezing my butt off, so I tried to be brief. Inside the house, the noise was incessant. My plan, though it didn't really exist, was to find someone who actually knew what was going on and could fix it. We would reconvene in a couple of weeks.

In order to leave the house, we had to walk past the basement door. As I got closer and the noise rang on, I had an inspiration. I opened the basement door and yelled, "Look, we're trying to help you, but you've gotta stop this and quit bothering these people, otherwise we can't."

I shut the basement door. In an instant, all the sounds stopped and silence surrounded us, but I had an eerie feeling while we bid our adieus and left for home.

I don't remember exactly what transpired on the way back, but I remember feeling like we'd climbed Mount Everest. What the heck was I going to do from here on?

CHAPTER 4

THE NEIGHBOR

In the coming week, I succumbed to the demands of my job and elected to move to a nice apartment in Jackson. While this placed me closer to work, so in good weather or bad, I would always be on time, it put me further away from my one and only ally in this fiasco. Barb was still working out of the same office, but her outstanding performance had made her a prime candidate for a promotion out of state. It appeared I would be on my own with not a single logical mind to discuss things with. The term up a creek without a paddle often came to mind. I wasn't afraid, but I was intimidated by the range of unknowns that lay before me. *Who would I call?* I didn't have a clue, so I literally did nothing on the haunted house for a couple of weeks.

I took a chance and asked my pastor about the house. He was cordial at first. Probably because I was a Sunday school teacher and sang in the choir.

"Satan's demons, Brett. I suggest you stay far away from there and pray for those folks. You don't know what evil lurks there. It could be your fastest way to HELL. I haven't seen you at the altar in a while. It might be a good idea to spend more time there than at the house."

"Pastor, there is nothing negative going on. These are religious people, and the spirit seems distressed. What about their children?"

The pastor was more direct. "Pray for them, Brett. Pray, but stay away."

"But pastor, didn't Jesus eat with the sinners and publicans? He wasn't afraid."

"You're not comparing yourself with Jesus Christ, are you?" he demanded as his tone of voice changed.

"No, but he was comfortable because he knew of his conviction to God. I know my conviction. No one is going to sway me away from my beliefs."

"This is blasphemy! Satan already has ahold of your heart." He blurted out.

It was obvious the pastor had no idea of who or what I was. I had promised my heart and my life to God, and I was 100% certain helping a distressed spirit would not change my philosophy. Because of the frustration I felt, I intentionally missed the next two Sunday services. If the pastor was so frightened at even the possibility of a spiritual presence, it obviously would not do me any good to talk with him further about it.

One evening I invited a friend and co-worker Kent to come and see my new apartment. That single request started a series of events that completely changed my life. As we approached the door to my building, I noticed another tenant walking towards the door, her hands laden with grocery bags. I decided it would be neighborly to hold the door open for her, while I took a moment to tell Kent about the haunted house.

As the lady passed, she asked. "Did I hear you say that you'd been to a haunted house?"

"Yes," I answered "Why?"

"If you wouldn't mind, I'd like to hear about it."

"Sure, I'm in apartment 202. Come on down."

I showed Kent around my apartment, and we took seats in the living room. In only a few minutes, there was a soft rap on the door. I opened it and welcomed Sandy into my humble abode.

"Tell me about the house." She began after we had completed introductions.

"Well, it's haunted by the spirit of a man that was murdered in the house."

During our greeting, Sandy told us she was an elementary school teacher, so I asked, "Why is this of interest to you?"

"Because I'm a spirit medium."

"What does that mean?"

"Oh, I'm sorry," she said. "A spirit medium is a person whose physical body is sensitive to vibrations not only of the physical world but also of the spirit realm."

"Which means what?"

"It means that we talk to dead people," she answered in a gentle tone.

Well, kiss my butt, I thought. Kent acted like he wasn't even listening, sitting quietly and staring into space.

"How did you learn how to do that?"

"Well, I read books, found a teacher, and began sitting in a séance circle."

"What the heck is a séance circle?"

"It's a group of people that get together every week and speak with spirits. We meet every Wednesday. Would you like to join us if we have an opening?"

I didn't know what to say; mediums, spirits, and séances. All a bit too much for me, but I thought it might be a way to help the folks in the haunted house.

"Sure, why not?"

"Ok, let me check with the group and I'll get back to you."

"Are you sure you want to do this?" Kent asked. He was always the voice of reason.

"Hell, I don't know, but what do I have to lose?"

The next day, when I came home from work, there was a note taped to my door that read - *Brett, stop up and see me in 301, Sandy.*

When I arrived, she opened the door slowly.

"So?"

"Well," she began, "bad news. The circle is full and there's no room to add anybody. They'll be starting a new circle in October. If you're still interested, you can join then."

"Thanks for checking anyway. I'll keep you posted on the house."

The door closed, and I returned to my own apartment. Bad news, indeed! It was only March. October was a lo-o-ong ways away. I didn't really think I'd still be interested then. Oh well, nothing ventured, nothing gained.

Two days later, on Friday, the forbearance of spring arrived. The temperature was in the 60s. The sun shone brightly, and I felt energized. To my surprise, there was a note taped on my door. Same message.

I knocked on Sandy's door, which opened almost at once. "Are you still interested?"

"Yeah, I guess so. Why?"

"One of our regulars had to quit. You can start next Wednesday if you like."

"Sounds great!" I exclaimed with a smile.

"Come in and let me give you some information. She told me the cross streets and wrote the address on a piece of paper. We start promptly at 7. Don't be late."

"Sandy, I'm a little uneasy. This is all new to me, and I'm not sure what to expect. Can you give me a little heads up?"

"Sure. Have you ever been to a Bible study at your church?"

I acknowledged I had.

"Well, it's a bit like that. We say a few affirmations, sing a song or two, and then greet the spirits as they come into our midst."

"Is it like Casper, the friendly ghost?"

Sandy laughed out loud. "No, no, no. Normally we don't see the spirits, we sense them. We'll explain more when we are all together. Trust me, there is absolutely nothing to be concerned about. I promise you'll love it."

Easy for you to say, I thought. I sure hoped she was right. My real purpose for going was to see if I could get some info that would help the family in the house.

CHAPTER 5

THE CIRCLE

Time passed quickly and before I knew it, I was driving out to Jackson for my first experience at a séance. I turned onto East Boulevard and drove for approximately two miles. In Jackson, that distance from the main road puts you in the boonies. I momentarily considered turning around, but then, I was still young and brave.

I pressed on. After another quarter of a mile, I came upon a small yellow bungalow with several cars parked nearby. I checked the address on the mailbox. I had arrived. Looking to my left and right, I noticed that the next closest house on either side was several hundred yards from this one. We were in the sticks. The inside front door to the house was open, so I headed in that direction.

As I neared the small porch of the house, the screen door swung open and an attractive middle-aged woman greeted me. "You must be Brett. Welcome."

"Thanks for having me," I replied.

"Glad to see you could make it," Sandy waved from inside the house.

It was greeting and meeting time. The lady who met me at

the door was Betty. Her husband, Al, reminded me of my dad, then there was Gary, an elementary school principal, and his wife Kathy, an older woman whom I immediately liked named Norma. The last in attendance were a middle-aged couple, Jeanie and Doug. What the heck was going on? I was the youngest person there by a long shot, and everyone seemed so normal. Doug had retired from Consumer's Energy and Al was a retired police officer. Jeanie was a retired paralegal from a law firm that was one of my sales accounts. In all, they were everyone's mom and dad, grandma or grandpa, and coworker. Where were the weird folks I had envisioned?

People were taking their seats in straight-backed chairs that were placed in a circle in the center of the living room.

"Norma is the séance leader," Sandy noted. "We alternate male and female, starting at her right."

I took a seat between Betty and Kathy. Everyone was taking off their shoes and placing them under their chairs. I followed suit.

The question on my face must have been obvious. Sandy leaned over. "It's to get a better grounding."

I nodded like I understood exactly what she was saying, though I honestly didn't have a clue. Thank goodness for clean socks.

Everyone scooted around a bit in their chairs, trying to get comfortable. Betty came in with a tray full of glasses filled with water. Each person took one, so I did, too. I took a sip from my glass and looked for a place to set it.

"No, don't drink it now. Place it under your chair and drink it afterward." Sandy divulged, "The spirit energy will ionize the water and it will refresh you."

I found a place under my chair next to my shoes and placed the glass there. Everyone else did likewise, and soon we were all sitting comfortably, waiting for the show to begin. I was suddenly very cold, though the temperature was warm. Betty turned the lights off and the room became as black as night. I literally couldn't see my hand in front of my face. I began to get nervous.

"Let's all say our affirmations," Norma began. She recited a phrase thanking spirit for guiding their group and asked for a blessing on the séance. One by one, each person in counter-clockwise fashion asked a blessing on themselves, others, and the circle.

I followed Norma's lead and thanked the spirits, whoever they were, for guiding me to the group and asked a blessing on myself and the circle. Even though I had no idea what I was doing, I felt better after saying the words. When everyone was finished, we simply sat there, not doing or saying anything for what seemed to be an eternity, which was really only about five minutes. I had kept my eyes closed, but during this brief break, I opened them. It was darker than I remembered. What next? I wondered.

Almost on cue, Norma began talking about people. "I Call Doctor Watson, Lillian Glazer, all of my guides, and any other spirits of truth or light that may wish to be recognized."

When it came to be my turn to call, I asked for my deceased brother Jim, my friend, Fred, and the spirit of the man at the house.

It pleased me when Kathy asked softly, "Have you sat in séance before?" She seemed surprised that I had not. Cha-ching, *I must be doing something right,* I thought.

Without further conversation, Norma began singing the Christian hymn, *In the Garden.* Everyone joined in. This song was one of my favorites and I knew the words well. We began singing the second verse. About halfway through, Norma coughed a deep cough, cleared her throat loudly, and sat straight up in her chair.

"Good evening, friends. This is Doctor Watson. I say

welcome to our guest, and hope that you will become a member of our group."

Okay, who the heck was Doctor Watson? *Why was Norma talking funny?* I thought. I hadn't heard her talk much, but the voice didn't sound like hers. This voice was deep and raspy.

Doctor Watson talked for perhaps fifteen minutes about world affairs and things we could expect to see in the next few weeks. Finally, he cleared his throat again and stated, "Until we meet again."

Betty rose and walked down a nearby hall where she turned on a light that only reflected a soft glow into the living room. Norma stirred and leaned forward. Betty reached under Norma's chair and handed her the water glass. Norma drank quickly, draining the glass.

I followed everyone's lead. The water tasted funny, but good. I drank it all and, as promised, I did feel better.

I replaced my shoes like everyone else and prepared to leave.

"Got time for coffee?" Norma asked me.

"If you're going, I'll be there. I have some questions."

"I'll bet you do," Norma chuckled. "Meet us at the Clock."

The Clock Restaurant was back down East Boulevard at Michigan Avenue.

"I'll see you there," I replied. Then thanked Betty and Al for having me and headed out.

The Clock was a traditional family-style restaurant, with breakfast served twenty-four hours a day and reasonable pricing. I took a seat at the head of a large group table and waited for the others.

When everyone arrived, Norma took a seat to my right. Laughing and talking, she broke out a smoke, lit her cigarette, and apologized. "Hope it doesn't bother you. It's my one real weakness."

Truth be told, I hated cigarette smoke since I quit, but I understood her addiction.

"It'll be alright," I answered.

Norma took a deep drag and held it for a long time before slowly exhaling. She then snuffed out the cigarette and ordered coffee and pie. A bit of dessert sounded like a good idea, so I ordered coffee and carrot cake.

"Nice to have you with us tonight. What did you think?"

I shrugged. "I guess I didn't understand it enough to have an opinion, but enjoyed it. It seems like something I'm supposed to do."

Norma laughed. "Oh, you're supposed to do it, alright. You don't choose it. It chooses you."

"So, who's Doctor Watson?"

Norma explained that Doctor Watson was one of her spirit guides and was her trance control, meaning that when she went into trance, Doctor Watson would use her body, or physical instrument as she called it, to communicate spiritual insights to the members of the group. She told me that some people call it channeling.

The cake and pie were gone. There had been several refills on the coffee, and I felt like I had the slightest inkling of an understanding of what had just taken place. Norma was patient and answered many of my questions. I wondered how something like this could have existed on the planet for so long, and regardless of my extensive research into religion, I had never heard of it.

"So, how do I get rid of the spirit in the house?"

"Simply ask it to leave. Offer reassurance that you will continue to investigate and promise that you will call for him when you have something concrete to report."

"That's it? It's as easy as that?"

"It is. If you have any problems, give me a call. Don't let it lay. Any info you can offer him will speed his departure."

As soon as I got home, I called Judy.

"Hello."

"It's Brett, I've got some good news," I announced.

"I could use some of that. What is it?"

"Tonight I went to an actual séance."

"You did?'

"Yes. It was a real, spirit talking, ghostly affair. I found out some neat things."

"Like what?"

"I want to tell you guys in person."

"Can our kids be here?"

"Sure. Nothing I'm going to talk about is scary. Did you find anything out about your house?"

"Yes, but not much."

"Do you know when it was built?"

"It looks like the early 1930s."

"Did you ever get a picture of the house as it looked originally?"

"No, but I'm still checking. Why?"

"I think after he was killed, they remodeled the house. I'll draw up a sketch."

We agreed to meet on Friday.

CHAPTER 6

1MPRESSIONS

hen the day came, I went solo and left the Tarot cards at home. Norma had convinced me I didn't need them to make contact. I trusted her wisdom.

Just from impressions, I had drawn up several sketches of what I thought the house looked like when it was built.

We again took our seats at the dining room table, with the children joining us. My decision to not invite Barb came back to haunt me as a wave of uncertainty swept over me, but she had not been at the séance nor talked to the facilitator or any of the other spirit mediums.

Over the next few minutes, I related what Norma had told me. As I finished, there was a soft knock on the basement door. Our spirit guest had obviously heard what I said.

I unfolded the sketches I had drawn. Fortunately, Judy had secured a completion photo of the house. *Bingo, it was a match.* The front roadside part, facing the street and side on the right of the house, had been completely changed.

"There was a fire," Judy reported. "Not a big one, but the owner remodeled after. They enlarged the size of the living room, added a fireplace, and widened the kitchen. In the basement, the cistern was removed and bricked up."

An eerie groan vibrated through the room and startled us all.

"You understand then?" I asked.

Three short taps responded.

"The original owner was killed in a car accident in 1969. The vehicle crashed and burned, killing him and his brother."

In the other room, the television turned on and off, confirming the spirit knew.

"So, what would you like us to do now?"

The house was quiet. I wasn't sure what to do, so I continued questioning.

"Now, will you feel enough peace to go home?"

I was hoping we were making progress, but again there was silence.

"What do you mean, go home?" Judy's daughter Erin asked with a confused look.

At only fourteen years old, Erin had great energy and a curious mind. I tried to seem experienced and not frighten her. "We humans come into a physical form from the spirit world. When we die, we go back to our original home. Our time as a physical person is a temporary state. We are spirit first and last."

"How do we know he's going to leave?" She responded.

I did my best to explain what Norma had told me. Everyone, even their young son, Mark, looked at me as if I had lost my mind.

I said with as much conviction as I could muster. "Once we help him, he should leave, and your house won't be haunted anymore."

Following Norma's direction, I encouraged the spirit to seek a tunnel of light and to walk towards it. Norma assumed that once he got in the vicinity of the light, he would know what to do. I added the affirmation that the spirit's time on Earth had expired and that a better life awaited him in the spirit world.

"I don't think he'll go," Erin mumbled.

"Why do you say that?"

"Cause I think he believes he lives here. It's creepy."

"You actually see him inside the house?" I asked.

"I do and my brother does, too. Tell him, Mark," she demanded.

I looked at the small face sitting to my right. "Is that true?"

He nodded slowly.

"I need to address this," I told everyone before posing the next question to the spirit. "Why are you doing this?"

Creaks were heard on the floor as if someone was walking on them.

The battle was far from over.

"But why?" Judy pleaded.

"You are not welcome here. Your time on Earth is finished." I stipulated.

The basement door opened wide, and then slowly closed with a slam. The temperature in the room dropped at least twenty degrees.

Everyone was moving around nervously in their chairs. I had a very unsettled feeling something was going to happen, and I didn't think it would be pleasant.

Time seemed to stop until Mark whispered, "Look."

He was pointing to the corner near the front door.

I turned quickly. There in the room's corner was a full apparition of a man with long hair and a beard. His image was translucent, but recognizable.

I braced myself. *Norma hadn't talked about any of this happening.*

Everyone was looking at me.

I didn't do it. As I finished the thought, there was a soft, whooshing sound. I began to tingle and blacked out.

When I opened my eyes, I was sitting in the most comfortable chair in a dimly lit room. Soft music played, and I was more relaxed than I could ever remember feeling. It seemed as if I should be sleeping, but I was wide awake.

Just as quickly as it started, I felt a sudden jerk. I was fully conscious and alert, sitting in a chair in Dylan and Judy's dining room.

Everyone was staring at me again, as if I had two heads.

"What?" I asked.

"Where did you go? It looked like you were in a trance." Dylan declared.

"Go? I didn't go anywhere. I guess I dozed off for a minute."

"Well," Judy began, "while you were dozing, the ghost image disappeared and your voice sounded funny."

"What did I say?"

"You talked about being remorseful. You said there would be no peace until the whole truth was uncovered."

"What?" I paused for a moment. "The spirit must have used my body as a vessel. I saw this happen at the seance to someone. It's called channeling."

"It definitely didn't seem like you." Dylan acknowledged.

The thought ran through my mind, *If the killer died in a car accident, how can we find more answers?* Of course, all of us were confused. I needed to talk to Norma.

The truth was that I wanted to run from the house as fast as I could and not look back. *I should have never gotten involved.* I didn't run, but as soon as I could get my ass moving, I was gone. It was near ten p.m. but I took the risk and gave Norma a call.

"How did it go?" she asked, hearing my voice.

"Not like I planned."

After a forty-five-minute discussion, I felt better, but my macho was way ahead of my logic. I wanted to go back to Judy's and give this spirit Hell, no pun intended.

Instead, I opted to call in the morning and set up another meeting. Norma believed that the spirit was stuck because the circle had not been closed. She sensed he was trying to stay because someone was still alive that was involved in his death. The lie was still alive. My first thought was the wife.

I called Judy the next morning. We agreed to meet the next evening at 7 o'clock.

"This time, could the children be in their bedrooms, please?"

"I think that's a wise idea. The last one was a bit much for them."

"Would you have any way of doing some research for me?"

"Sure, what did you have in mind?"

I explained that if we could find out the names of the owners who died in the crash, it might lead us to the wife. We could at least update the spirit on her status, and that might encourage him to leave.

CHAPTER 7

THE OWL

Sunday came quickly, and right at 7:00 we were sitting at the dining room table.

Judy provided some new information. "Franco and Marcello DeNunzio, owned one of the largest construction companies in Michigan. In November of 1969, when they died in the car accident, Franco's wife, Frieda, the lone surviving family member, closed out their affairs and moved to Redwood City, California. In 1970, the last known address was 1321 Cumberland, apartment 34."

"Great research! Now perhaps I can find her and have her fess up to the affair so we can get things back to normal."

"Can you hear us?" I asked into the room.

There were several bangs on the basement door.

"We have a lead on the wife."

The chimes outside started rattling and I presumed it was in response to my statement.

"Is that why you're staying?"

A gust of wind blew the door open, and a shiver went down my spine. Judy moved quickly to close it.

I asked, "Was that you?"

A buzzing sound filled the air like a bumble bee in flight.

"By the way, what did they do with your body once they closed the cistern? Were you buried?"

Silence.

"Did they cremate you?"

Several rapid knocks like an in-law at the door.

"Are your ashes in the house?"

Loud booms began on the furnace pipes and continued.

"Is that a sore spot for you?"

One of the dining room chairs slid three feet to the right and stopped suddenly, almost falling over.

The pieces were coming together. At least, I thought they were.

"Here's what I think. He's mad because the wife could have saved him but didn't. He was cremated and something disrespectful was done with his remains. If we can get some info on the wife and perhaps find his ashes and dispose of them properly, your troubles may be over."

"Look," Judy pointed with a gasp. "The owl is in the center of the floor again."

"Damn it," I yelled. "You've got to stop doing that."

I walked to the owl and grabbed it by the head in order to pick it up and return it to the stereo. When I did, the head came off in my hand. I was left looking down into the hollow neck of the owl. Almost as quickly as I regained my composure, a large swarm of flies flew out and began buzzing over the statue, then began dying and falling to the floor. They lay like black stones on Judy's light-colored carpet. I jumped back when the head came off, but now leaned forward to look inside. I wanted to throw up. The whole bottom of the owl was filled with maggots, thousands of them.

"Did you cut this off?" I asked Dylan.

"No way, I haven't touched it. In fact, it's not even ours. We found it in the closet when we moved in."

The cut was smooth, as if done by a laser. The edges were beveled and safe to the touch. On further examination, I attested we had found the remains of our disembodied spirit.

All that was left now was to locate Freida. I opted to use some frequent flier miles and take a trip to California. Redwood City is just southwest of San Francisco. I caught the red eye, hoping to find Mrs. DeNunzio after breakfast.

Fortunately, the plane was not crowded. There were plenty of seats and lots of elbow room. The flight was smooth, and just after 6:30 in the morning the wheels touched down at San Francisco International Airport. The Avis counter was empty except for one agent who appeared to have been awake all night. After signing a few forms and locating my destination on a map, I was on my way.

My stomach called to me, so I stopped and purchased a breakfast sandwich and a coffee. I figured I would need my strength for the next phase of discovery. After depositing my trash in the bin, I was back on the road for the short ride to the Golden Gate Apartments.

Number 34 was on the ground floor at the far end of the two-story structure, away from the parking lot. I knocked softly and heard stirring inside. After a few moments, the door cracked open ever so slightly and a short-haired woman with glasses peered through the opening.

"Yes?"

"Frieda DeNunzio?"

"Who wants to know?"

I briefly explained who I was, but didn't tell her the purpose of my visit.

The door swung open and Frieda stepped back to allow my entry.

"Come in."

I stepped into the small apartment and looked around.

Frieda closed the door, and I immediately noticed how dark the room had become.

"Please sit down," she offered, pointing to a chair and a sofa. Frieda took a seat opposite me on the other side of the coffee table that sat in the center of the room.

"I'm here to talk about your husband and brother-in-law."

"They're both dead," she exclaimed as her forehead wrinkled.

"I know, but I need to talk about the events that occurred just before their deaths."

"Like what?"

"The affair." I whispered cautiously.

"What affair?" she uttered.

"The one you were having that caused the death of an innocent man."

"Oh, he wasn't innocent. Charles was as hot to trot as all of them. I didn't always look like this and he was relentlessly trying to seduce me, but I just wasn't interested."

Frieda rose and walked into the bedroom area. When she returned, she handed me a picture of a voluptuous woman with a bright smile and long black hair.

As I looked at the picture, I asked, "Who was Charles?"

"Charles Summers was our maintenance man and too damn nosy for his own good. Franco had lost his flair, if you know what I mean. His brother, Marcello, was young and strong. He was a lover. Coulda had any woman he wanted, but he picked me. I assumed Franco wouldn't know the difference anyway, so I decided not to deprive myself any longer. As the days went on, our meetings became more and more frequent and less clandestine. One day when we were in the thick of it, Charles came into the room. The next day he told me that if I didn't sleep with him, he was gonna tell Franco.

"So, he was blackmailing you?"

"Yes."

Just then a picture of her, Franco, and Marcello fell off the wall and crashed to the floor causing her to flinch and clasp her chest. She was visibly shaken and I wondered if Charles had joined me on the trip.

When she'd calmed down a bit, I reworded my question. "Are you sure he was blackmailing you?"

She looked me straight in the eyes and gave a long pause. "Actually no, but I told Marcello he was, hoping he could convince Charles to leave me alone."

"Unfortunately, Marcello's reaction was more than I bargained for and a few days later, he told me our problems were over. Franco never knew why Charles disappeared. He presumed he took a better job elsewhere. Plus, my husband traveled a lot for business and left Marcello in charge of the remodeling. During the construction, Marcello told a friend who owned a funeral home and crematorium that he found a body buried in the cistern. The mortician agreed to take care of the problem for a fee, allowing Marcello and I to continue our meetings right up until the day they were killed."

"So, Charles died needlessly, because of a lie?"

"I guess you could say that, but he wasn't just an innocent bystander. He shouldn't have kept trying to pursue me after I told him no, but I wouldn't have misled Marcello if I knew what he was going to do. The guilt has been eating at me and I've been worried this day might come. My remaining years have been lonely and riddled with health problems. Now I'm dying. The doctors have given me less than six months to live. Looking back, I wish I had done things differently. Charles might still be alive."

The puzzle was complete.

The flight back to Michigan was uneventful. I was eager to get home and call Judy and Dylan.

I was hopeful we could finally bring an end to this macabre story.

When we met again, I gave them a recap.

"I have a feeling Charles not only wanted his remains to be discovered, but the truth along with them. Hopefully, he can rest since Frieda is dying and admitted her guilt."

"Charles, did you hear that?"

Three quick clangs resounded through the house.

"We're going to hold a service and spread your ashes over the lake."

Another positive response.

Dylan and Judy had a beautiful pontoon boat, so after our meeting, I picked up the owl and we took a slow turn around the lake. A soft spring mist was falling around us. The sky was brilliant with shades of pink and orange as the sun worked its way into the west.

We found a beautiful spot with a cove of trees near the water's edge, I said a prayer for Charles' spiritual progression, and asked forgiveness for his human indiscretions. As we cruised, the lake became the final resting place for the remains of Mr. Charles Summers. When at last the owl was empty, I asked Dylan to drive to the center. Then I dropped the statue and head into the water and watched them slowly disappear from view. With our task complete, we turned towards shore and witnessed a bright rainbow appear above the lake. A clear sign that Charles had gone home.

THANK YOU FOR READING *HAUNTED*. We hope you enjoyed it! If you'd like to continue The Starlite Supernatural Mystery Series, you can read our standalone shorts in any order.

BOOKS 2 READ

https://books2read.com/ap/nA7AdP/Ray-and-Michele-Fraser

ILLUSTRATION

TAROT CARD ILLUSTRATION

Years ago, there was only one set of Tarot cards available - the Rider Waite deck.

Today, there are hundreds of varieties to suit the reader, each one with different illustrations but similar meanings.

INSPIRED BY

For those of you who are curious, this story is based on true events that Ray experienced early in his spiritual development. He has spent his career helping people, so this chance meeting was obviously destiny. If you'd like to learn more about his unfoldment/awakening, watch for Ray's memoir, coming out in 2024.

Author Notes

Thank you for reading our story.
We love hearing your feedback, so we hope you'll post a review.

If you liked *Haunted*, please check out our other
Starlite Supernatural Mysteries.

Receive an exciting look into *Mary* by signing up for our
newsletter using the Bookfunnel link below.
https://dl.bookfunnel.com/xpkhinq30n

Plus, get behind the scenes tidbits and learn about new releases.

Mary
A young girl with a mysterious background sets off an
investigation into the dark reaches of time.

<u>Reviews</u>

Mary

"A short paranormal novella that's just about ninety pages long:
I enjoyed every aspect of it. I wished it was longer, but just
because I loved the writing style - the characters. The flow of
the book was just perfection. Also, I liked the action part at the
beginning and the mystery each chapter brought. It never had a
dull moment."
- <u>Midnightstorybook</u>

Mary

"Read it as an ARC. Absolutely loved this story. Held my
attention the whole time. The plot was consistent from
beginning to end. Gave off a murder mystery vibe without
murder. No cliffhangers with a great unexpected ending.
Suspenseful and mysterious. Definitely worth reading if you
want to try out the supernatural mystery genre."
- <u>Elizabeth S.</u>

Mary

"Every time I thought I had an idea of who Mary was and where
she came from, I'd learn about new piece of the puzzle and have
to throw all my theories out the window. Things get stranger as
the story progresses, which just made me more eager to figure
out what was really going on. I felt a bit bad for our main
character Jason and his quest to return Mary to her family, but I
admired how determined he was to help such an odd little girl.

For such a brief story, "Mary" is packed full of intrigue and
mystery - who is this little girl, where is she from, and why
doesn't she understand how to drink a milkshake? I can
guarantee you won't see the answer coming!

I really enjoyed this read, and I'd recommend it to anyone looking for a novella that will keep them guessing. I'm looking forward to reading more by Ray and Michele Fraser - thank you so much to the authors for the opportunity to read this book!"
- Anna

ALSO BY RAY & MICHELE

If you enjoyed this Starlite Mystery, check out our other unique spellbinding shorts. They're the perfect escape when you're pressed for time.

The Starlite Supernatural Mystery Series:

Haunted

The Wind

The Promise

Mary

1421 Maple

Sarah

Coming Soon

Enter the web of intrigue, suspense, and danger in

The Sean Thomas Paranormal Mystery Series

Book 1 - *A Switch in Time*

For a complete list of Ray and Michele's books

or

to request signed paperbacks visit our website.

www.rayandmichelefraser.com

About the Authors

Ray and Michele are a full-time writing team with a serious passion for storytelling. They combine their love of writing, vivid imagination, and years of experience as professional spirit mediums to guide their readers into uncharted territories.

In 1994, Ray's intuitions fostered by Cherokee and Scottish ancestry, led him to open Mystiques-West Metaphysical Center in Michigan. During the twenty-three years of operation, Ray hosted a #1 radio talk show and a live TV show, called "The Mystical Connection." They performed home cleansing, organized ghost hunts, taught classes in mediumship, and led weekly public seances to connect clients to their departed loved ones on the other side. The messages from spirit have helped many to find peace. Ray also facilitated the last four National Houdini Seances sponsored by Houdini historian Sid Radner.

In addition to readings and life coaching sessions, Ray's work as an ordained minister has provided his clientele with years of grief and relationship counseling, weddings, and funerals.

As a screenwriter, Michele brings her love of film into the fold by incorporating her own style of creativity into their endeavors. She's also the backbone of the editing process, social media management, cover design, and marketing.

Ray and Michele infuse their stories with mystery, intrigue, tales of the afterlife, and other worldly phenomena to create a fascinating and adventurous journey for readers.

For more info - linktr.ee/RayandMicheleFraser

Ray's extensive background and keen storytelling abilities combined with Michele's love of screenwriting and editing has made them a powerhouse duo.
www.rayandmichelefraser.com

DON'T MISS OUT

Click the button below to sign up for our fan exclusive newsletter to get behind the scenes tidbits and learn about new releases.

There's no charge or obligation,
and we never sell your information.

https://rayandmichelefraser.com/newsletter

BOOKS 2 READ

https://books2read.com/ap/nA7AdP/Ray-and-Michele-Fraser

WHAT PEOPLE ARE SAYING

The Wind

"This book ensnared me from the get-go. Like the wind whispering encouragement to keep on reading. The fact that the writers are able to create such a wonderfully thrilling story within such few pages is pure magic. It kept me on my toes and I read the whole thing in one sitting. I genuinely believe this could be adapted into a full length novel.

Character development was great especially for a novella and the storyline was stella.

I would highly recommend this, and during the start it was giving me major Phantom vibes by Dean R Koontz and he is one of my all time favs in the thriller department.

If you like thrillers, or wives tales or simply short stories then this is the book for you, even if you only said yes to one of those."
- Juniper Raven

The Promise

"Just finished reading this story... and I am blessed beyond words! It's a beautiful paranormal novella focusing on grief, loss, sadness, and ultimately - redemption. For lovers of *Chicken Soup for the Soul* books and the *Sixth Sense* film, you will be delighted to have the time to read this short story - and feel compelled to engage in the entire series! Thank you to @rayandmichelefraser for the wonderful opportunity to share

this story of mystery and intrigue with you all! I highly
recommend and rate it 5 of 5 sweet stars!"
- Deb

Mary

"I went into this novella only knowing that it was described as a
paranormal mystery. I love paranormal books but I don't read
mystery too often so I was interested to see how these two
genres combined. Immediately as the story began I was
interested in discovering who exactly this mysterious Mary
was. I thought I had an idea as to where things were going and
who Mary was but I was so wrong! I don't want to spoil
anything, but when Jason started digging up the past I certainly
didn't expect the story to go where it did. This was a quick yet
captivating read that I'd recommend if you're a fan of either
paranormal or mystery."
- MissS3LFD3STRUKT

1421 Maple

"I really enjoyed this short story! It's one of those thrillers that
you can finish on a lunch break and feel like you spent 45
minutes in an alternate universe. I was intrigued from the
beginning, but a plot twist came around and I had to keep
reading to see what was going on. Perfect for those just getting
into a thriller genre!"
- Brenna P., Outreach Librarian

Sarah

"This is a page turner. Sarah finds herself in a destructive marriage that is not at all what she thought she was getting into. Charlie is charming on the outside with an evil heart. To survive, she had to do something drastic. But will she ever be truly free from her torturing husband? Fans of A Tell Tale Heart will find this an interesting twist on a classic story."

- Brook